Other works of fiction by Robert Kelly

The Scorpions

The Cruise of the Pnyx

A Transparent Tree

Doctor of Silence

Cat Scratch Fever

Queen of Terrors

The Logic of the World

The Collected Stories

Robert Kelly

SHADOW TALK

Twenty-five New Fairy Tales

With drawings by

Emma Polyakov

McPherson & Company
Kingston, New York

2021

McPherson & Company
P.O. Box 1126 Kingston, NY 12402
WWW.MCPHERSONCO.COM
Typeset in Mrs Eaves and Mr Darcy.
Design by Bruce R. McPherson.
1 3 5 7 9 10 8 6 4 2 2021 2022
Printed in U.S.A.

Library of Congress Cataloging-in-Publication Data

Names: Kelly, Robert, 1935- author. | Polyakov, Emma O'Donnell, illustrator.
Title: Shadow talk : twenty-five new fairy tales / Robert Kelly ; with drawings by Emma Polyakov.
Description: Kingston, New York : McPherson & Company, 2021.
Identifiers: LCCN 2021031330 | ISBN 9781620540466 (trade paperback)
Subjects: LCGFT: Fairy tales.
Classification: LCC PS3521.E4322 S43 2021 | DDC 813/.54—dc23
LC record available at https://lccn.loc.gov/2021031330

Note

A limited autograph edition of ten of these stories was issued in 2019 under the title *Ten New Fairy Tales*. That book has been expanded for this first trade edition by the addition of fifteen illustrated tales and an introduction by the author.

I offer these tales
in Loving Memory of my First Instructors

MARGARET ROSE KELLY, née KANE

1902–1990

SAMUEL JASON KELLY

1900–1990

CONTENTS

Tales

A TALE is anything told. A fairy tale is something told . . . by fairies? About fairies? Pretending to be about fairies? The *contes de fée* that give us the phrase, equally ambivalent — or, to be Empsonian about it, polybolous. Meaning many things at once.

I dare to use the word because *Fairy* is to me the normal word for the Whisperers in forests, the voice over waters, you know they're near by the way you shiver, or feel a kind of curious fear that instead of making you run away makes you linger, go closer. So for me one of the many meanings of that sweet old word is *what tells itself in your head when you look at a tree, or running stream, or just look out the window of your house with nothing on your mind.*

I certainly pray I do not use the word falsely or illicitly. I tell what they tell me, and I tell you. That's the simplest way to say it, even if neither of us knows who *they* are.

○ ○ ○

The tales, by good fairy logic, had the good fortune to catch the eye of Emma O'Donnell Polyakov, an artist and historian of religion whose astonishing study of liturgy, *Remembering the Future*, had caught my mind.

When she offered to illustrate the first collection of these tales, I was delighted, shocked at how her awareness of the savage simplicity of religions could carve images that say so much.

○ ○ ○

When I was a little boy my father used to sing: *All night around the fairy tree / the little people play / and men and women passing / turn their heads away / But if your heart's a child's heart...*

Let me hope so.

RK, April 2021

SHADOW TALK

The Fox and the Other Side

FOR several years there was a fox's den behind our summerhouse. A foxes' house I should say, because the den was home to a red fox at some times, a black fox at others. I had never seen a black fox.

I used to sit screened in, sprawled in a big old armchair, safe from the mosquitoes of eventide, insistent as church bells. I wanted to see the black fox close up, but never managed to do so. Only when I was far across the lawn would he appear, moving slow enough for me to see him clearly, but not too clear.

Anyhow, I liked the red fox better, it was a real foxy fox, color of marmalade, color of cream, with a sly gait and a furtive glance here and there — he knew how to be a fox, looking like a four-foot version of any high school student slouching home.

I read up on foxes and found that there

were black foxes, green foxes, and blue foxes as well as the ordinary kind they called 'rufous' though red would do well enough. "These are," I read in the big nature book, "the foxes of the other side. Watch out for them. When they appear they sometimes seize the territory of the rufous or common fox. There are known instances, furthermore, where the apparition of a black fox has heralded, or perhaps even induced, changes in the visual apparatus of human spectators, so that ever after one color seems suddenly much (as one patient described it) 'louder than before, louder than it ought to be.' Such examples of chromatic peril are not uncommon in the tropics, but rare in North America."

The next time I saw the black fox I closed my eyes right away, and called out to him,

Why do you change our eyes? To my surprise, he answered lucidly, in an accent that reminded me of a friend of my wife from Slovenia: I change you to make you see the other side – that's where I come from and where you are going. Get ready.

After silence, I opened my eyes. No fox. I walked over to the summerhouse, over grass that seemed preposterously green.

The Witch and the Well

LONG AGO, all the people in the town knew that the widow woman who lived all alone in a little cottage beyond the last field that anybody plowed was a witch. She wasn't very old, because her husband had gone off to be a soldier and died in a war they were having at the time. But she lived alone and that was strange. And she never came into town if she could help it, and that was even stranger. So she must be a witch, and was so called, and people did not scruple to name her a witch even when speaking aloud to friends and family.

That is how young Thaddeus came to know that the widow woman was a witch. He didn't know much about witches, just enough to be afraid. So when one day he was walking along the road on the edge of town, on his way to an old pear tree on nobody's land, cranky old tree, but it still bore sweet pears now and then, especially if you came by in late winter or earliest spring and whacked the trunk of it with a stick to wake up the juice inside the tree.

As he walked along, he noticed the witch's cottage ahead to his left, and knew he'd have to pass it to get to his tree. He hastened his steps, and he was in a hurry anyhow, to get to the tree before other people had stripped it bare — so he didn't have to think he was hurrying just out of fear of the witch lady.

But as he hurried past the rickety fence in front of her yard, sure enough the witch was there, looking right at him, and she called out to him by name. How did she know his name? He guessed that witches knew things like that, knew somebody's name just by looking at them.

She called him again, and though he didn't at all want to go to her, his feet had other ideas, and he started moving to the witch. He came through the little gate, which was open and no door in it at all, and came close to the woman. She smiled at him and said,

"Thaddeus, I have some water for you. Some special water. Come have a drink."

She turned her back and went over to the well in the yard, canopied by old wood, tree limbs with the bark still on them. She turned her back to him and bent over the well, and seemed to be hauling up a bucket of water. Special water, Thaddeus thought, and was very afraid.

Like most children, he had been taught, or somehow learned, to hate witches, to throw stones at them if you could do it without them seeing. He had heard stories of people killing their cats or even setting fire to their houses. Thaddeus didn't think that was a right thing to do, even to a witch, but he was very afraid, and his fear made him do something he probably would not have done. He rushed at the witch with all his force and pushed her into the well.

But she didn't go into the well. She wasn't even there. Thaddeus had passed right through the image of her body and kept going, and it was he who fell into the well. And there he lay, stunned. The well was not deep as he thought, and he had fallen only a couple of feet, just enough to have the breath knocked out of him. And there was no water in the well, just soft earth, and flowers growing densely in the shadow. Blue flowers of a kind he'd never seen. He lay there, confused but oddly happy, snuggled down in the flowers.

When he looked up, he could see the round dark roof of the well, and all the daylight around it. As he watched, the witch's face appeared. She looked down at him, smiling still.

"Do you like my water, Thaddeus, my son? I told you it was special. How do you like it?"

He couldn't imagine why she called him her son, but he thought the least he could do would to be polite, considering what he had done. Or tried to do. Or had he done anything at all?

"It is very pleasant here, missus. The flowers are very pretty."

"I'm glad you like them," said the witch. "They only grow where the sun can't hurt them, and my special water keeps them moist and happy. Now would you like to try my special bread? I baked it just for you. It tastes of honey and of pears, and I know you like pears."

Thaddeus was not altogether a dull child, so he thought out loud: "If I can't drink your special water, but only lie in it, will I be able to eat your special bread?"

The witch smiled again. This time her smile seemed sweet and loving, full of the sunshine. He could feel the flowers around him shivering with worry at all that gleaming. She smiled and smiled and said, "O dear son, you already have. My bread is in your body now, and you will never forget me."

Then she was gone. Thaddeus waited a little while to see if she'd come back, or if anything else was going to happen. But nothing did, so he stood up and climbed easily enough out of the well. When he got onto the grass of the yard, he looked back into the well, and now all he could see was water, dark water down there, and his own face looking back up at him.

People in the town never saw the witch again. Her house stood empty for many a year, shunned by those who should have known better. But Thaddeus would come visiting from time to time, even sit in the witch's old chair and light a fire in her hearth, always easy to kindle and quick to catch. As he grew older he grew more learned, and eventually became the town physician and general authority on this and that, a quiet, grave man who never married.

And once when the King passed through the neighborhood, it was in Thaddeus's house he stopped for a cup of cider and a slice of bread, and the men looked at one another like people who had known one another long ago, but couldn't be sure.

The Ape and the Antelope

ONCE upon a time there lived an ape and an antelope. The time is actually now, and they live in different countries but they know how to talk to each other, using a scientific principle awaiting detection: sciosophy, they call it, the wisdom of shadows. Seems that if you dance around and make shadows of a certain sort and in a certain order, the air picks the shadows up as signals which can be decoded anywhere on the planet by those in the know. The ape (in Namibia) and the antelope (in Wyoming) were two such cognoscenti, who'd gotten to know and trust each other (what harm could one do to other?) some years before during a partial eclipse of the moon, partial in Africa, total in the West. They had much to talk about, each describing at length the customs and obstacles of their region.

One day the antelope had a run-in with some hunters, thickish white men in colorful warm coats. She liked the colors but was afraid. When they began shooting at her, she ran away and hid in a little ravine, where she urgently shadowed a message to her friend the ape.

"When they're white, run away," the ape explained.

"I did that, I'm hiding now, what should I do?"

"Well, you can run fast but bullets run faster, I can't run much myself, so try to outsmart them. Try this: repeat the following formula while striking the earth with your, let's see, right forefoot: *Agamagus Hariganus Farnabayus Hilderskoot*. At the last syllable, toss your horns in the air — you do have horns, don't you?"

"They're small, I'm a girl."

"Well, any size will do. You know the formula?"

Animals are very good at remembering, since they don't have books to scatter their memories. So the antelope said Yes, but asked the ape to repeat it one more time. The ape did so, and the antelope mouthed the syllables to fix them in mouth.

Then she stood up and bellowed the phrase,

AGAMAGUS HARIGANUS
FARNABAYUS HILDERSKOOT

while she pounded the hard-packed winter earth.

An eighth of a mile away, one of the hunters got a sudden toothache, and recalled that he had accidentally skipped his scheduled visit to the dentist. And the other hunter, with equal suddenness, remembered an appointment in town, an important one, money was involved. So both hunters turned around and went home.

Antelope and ape shared their pleasure, the antelope promising to think of some way to be of help to the ape, the ape, embarrassed, saying no need for that. But it is fortunate, isn't it, that humans have such poor memories.

Green Silk

EMMA loved to walk in the big meadow after breakfast, even on days like today, with grey clouds all over the sky, only a little blue showing through. On the far side of the meadow, where the land rose gently, she saw a figure motionless. Curious. The field is usually empty in this season. Emma decided to investigate.

When she got closer, she could see that there was a woman sitting on the grass, her back against a boulder. Emma didn't recall a boulder being there, but there it was.

The woman was reading a book. She was wearing a big sunhat despite the day being so overcast, but then Emma noticed that the woman was sitting in a little patch of sunlight — that must help her read. The woman was wearing a big pair of tortoise-shell framed eyeglasses, and was holding the book close to her face, so Emma couldn't see her well. The most striking thing was how she was dressed: in a long, long dress of green silk that lay smooth along her outstretched legs.

Emma wondered about the book; she liked books a lot, had a few dozen of her own at home, so she came close to have a look. The woman lowered the book, though, and looked up, smiling at Emma. Emma really wanted to ask what she was reading, but all at once felt shy, so said instead something about how beautiful the dress was.

Would you like to feel it, the woman asked. Emma didn't especially want that, but felt it would be polite to say yes, yes is always polite, isn't it? So she bent forward and touched the silk as the woman raised one knee to meet her touch.

The cloth was soft and good to feel, and it shifted a little lightly on the skin beneath it. And as it moved, suddenly Emma felt very dizzy, toppled sideways, was being carried along, what was happening, suddenly she was in a stream pouring down the slope, there was no stream in the meadow but now there was and she was in it, tumbling, slipping along, the water too shallow to swim in, but deep enough to carry a young girl along.

Then she stopped flowing. She lay there looking at the sky a moment to catch her breath. Then she got up.

There was no stream there, no woman up there on the slope, no boulder. But Emma was soaking wet, water from her hair dripping past her eyes as she looked around.

It began to rain, hard, and Emma was glad because now she wouldn't have to explain how she got drenched. She ran home to dry off and put on dry clothes. As it happened, no one noticed when she came dripping in, so she dried off and everything was back to normal — outside, at least, but there was much wonder in her mind.

The rest of the day was like any day in summer, nothing happened but took a long time doing it. Emma read her books but kept drifting away from the story into thinking about what had happened. Did she imagine a stream? Did she become a stream? It was all very confusing, so she played with the cat instead, and went out to feed the chickens.

The next morning a delivery van pulled up at the door of their house, and a nice man in a brown uniform brought a package up the steps, handed it to Emma who loved being the one who got the mail and deliveries.

The package was soft and thick, wrapped in brown paper. To her surprise, the address on the package just said Emma, nothing more.

She tore the wrapping off and there was a green silk dress. She ran upstairs, undressed and tried the dress on. It fit perfectly, reached just to her ankles.

As she twirled to study herself in the mirror, she noticed a piece of paper taped to the back of the dress. She reached round and pulled it free and read what it said: You can be me too.

Emma was thrilled and frightened. What could that mean? She waited that night till everyone was asleep, put the dress on and went outside, not all the way across the meadow but right near her house, just in

case. She lay down and stroked the cloth along her leg just as she had done. And she began to flow, smoothly, softly, no confusion now, no tumbling, just a pure sweet current of ongoingness.

But this was different — when she stood up after a few minutes of flow, she was completely dry, the dress unruffled, her hair neat. She had flowed half across the meadow, and it took a few minutes to walk home.

So for years and years Emma would put on the dress from time to time and flow. Sometimes on the meadow, sometimes in the forest, and once even on a deserted street in a city on a trip to Europe. All through the years, the dress grew with her, always fit her perfectly no matter how tall she grew.

The Boy in the Camel

ONCE upon a time a boy was born inside a camel. No one knew why. As he grew, the boy learned to make his way around, first in the animal, then later, as the animal when it moved around in the world.

Sometimes the boy slipped his little legs into the big front legs of the camel, sometimes into the hind legs, and so learned to walk. If he had had language already, he would have said I walk twice. But as it was, he just walked.

And there was plenty of room in the hump for his head. So as he grew, he never felt squeezed in or uncomfortable. Though it is only honest to remark that he never liked the food the camel give him, though the water the animal gulped up was tasty, and helped him tolerate the bland food. He became

after a while something of a connoisseur of water — springs, oases, lakes, rivers, standing pools, he knew them all.

His years passed pleasantly enough, travelling about, walking, trotting, or all curled up asleep under the hump, cradle-rocked by the camel's gentle lurching. The camel taught him Camelese (with a heavy Saharan accent) and the boy taught the camel a language he thought was Humanish that he had made up, so the two got on well together. The boy had no idea that there were other humans, or if there were, that some of them might live outside their camel. The camel, though, in chatting with his kin and kind, suspected that few other camels had boys living inside them. It made him feel very special indeed, but he was careful not to let on to the boy how unusual their situation was. And he never disclosed it to other camels either, or anybody else, until one fine day he came to the oasis called El Fna.

There he found a great wodge of freshly cut khat, a mild intoxicant leaf for humans that causes dimmed wits and sharpened dreams, people like dullness with pictures in it, so khat is popular. Strange to find so much of it just lying there. But so he did, and gobbled it all right up. Almost at once, the inside boy fell fast asleep and dreamed about stars and stones and bowls of milk. But the camel got very excited, danced around and started bellowing this and that, old camelish jokes and puns and bawdy songs. When he trotted up to a pond nearby and spread his legs to bend to drink, he saw his own form mirrored in the water, and cried out, O most beautiful travel camel, how sprint and springy thy leaping about, how graceful thy formy-warm, who would know a talking boy lives all inside?

Now as it happened a Djinn was passing overhead at the moment, and as usual paying no attention to the clamor drunk or sober of camels — until the last part of the camel's boast.

Hm, thought the Djinn, a talking boy. I could use one of those. And with deft, magic, long, many-jointed djinn-fingers he painlessly opened the camel's side, plucked out the still-sleeping boy, zipped up the camel, told the animal O you're better off this way, tucked the boy under his wing and flew away.

It didn't take the boy long to get used to his new life, but he never did get used to the bright daylight. Historians credit him with the invention of sunglasses. His gait was peculiar, even as a grown man, lurching, abruptly swooping down a little at the waist. He became a scholar and writer, famous in Arabic literature as Abd el-Batn, servant of the interior, master of esoteric lore.

The Girl Who Could Change

ONCE there was a girl who could change into other things.

Or so she said, but very few people believed her. And she was mostly content to be amused by their skepticism, and never tried to persuade them of her skill.

Since she was six years old she had possessed, or said she possessed, this ability to change into other things. She'd mention it to people casually, the way she'd describe herself as a Methodist or confess to being fond of cherry-cheesecake. She soon stopped mentioning it to people, either because they scoffed or were silenced with embarrassment. But she could change if she wanted to, she knew.

It was different, though, with one boy she met in her class in junior high. He wasn't much to look at, wrote poetry, listened to weird music, and was probably Jewish. But he was a serious boy, and looked at her often, and spoke politely to her. Sometimes they walked part of the way home together. One day, she mentioned, in passing, that she could change into other things.

David nodded, unsmiling, looked as if he had suspected it all along.

"Could you change into a wolf?" he asked.

"I don't like wolves," she said,

"How about a horse . . . could you be a horse?"

"No problem," she said. "Just turn around and close your eyes."

"Why can't I watch?"

"Because I have to take off all my clothes — otherwise they'd get torn apart when I get so big."

So David turned his back and closed his eyes, though he thought that turning away was enough. Behind him he heard the soft noise of clothes being moved, removed. And then a loud snort.

He turned round and there she was, a big horse, reddish brown, with a paler mane, and big eyes looking at him.

"That's fantastic" he cried, "you really are a horse! How does it feel?"

She was silent. He asked again, and then if she was ok, and still silent. The horse kept looking at him, and then he realized, of course, a horse can't talk. He patted the muzzle of the horse, and she accepted his affectionate gesture.

Then David, who liked to go to the zoo, and to read books about wild animals, thought of how beautiful leopards and panthers are. Before really thinking it out, he asked, "Can you change into a panther?"

Instantly the horse swirled down, its legs shortened, body lengthened, muzzle shortened, eyes turned green. And there was a black panther looking at him. Mild eyes, but so lithe and fierce the body. And finally David was afraid. He wanted to pat the sleek dense fur of the animal, but that was too frightening to consider.

"Oh please change back to yourself, you're wonderful, come back, come back!"

The panther just looked at him. She nodded her head once. But did nothing more.

He waited.

She growled, gently, and nodded her head again. David caught on—she wanted him to turn away again so she could change back into her clothes and be a girl again. So he turned his back and closed his eyes, half-expecting the animal would pounce on him and claw or bite. It was a scary moment for David indeed.

Then he heard a clothy sound, and something that sounded like human breath, then heard the unmistakable sound of a zipper being zipped up.

He turned round and there she was, his friend, smiling at him, proudly, the way a gymnast looked at the school gym after carrying out some exploit. A little out of breath, a big smile.

He threw his arms around her and hugged her tight, telling her she was wonderful, and so on, sort of babbling, but excited now, almost breathless, as if he himself had done the deed.

She calmed him down, and they walked away, back out of the park into the street, hand in hand for a block or so, till they got a little nervous and let each other go.

The Umbrella

ONCE upon a time, and not so very long ago at that, a traveler was making his way west from Bengal, and was crossing the flat fields of Bihar, which was then and likely still is now, the poorest state in India. As he pedaled along, he reflected that for a country with a population of a billion India could manage at times to look deserted. Here, for instance, with jungly places on the left and rice fields to the right, the road straight and empty, our traveler hadn't seen a soul in half an hour of conscientious cycling.

All the more surprising to see, upright, open and unfurled, a gentleman's umbrella standing straight up out of the muddy paddy. This was no parasol or beach umbrella, this was a black silken affair such as a rich businessman in Kolkata would shield him-

self with on his way in drizzle from the bank to the club. An umbrella standing up in an empty field. A mystery. Our traveler was intrigued, and wheeled his bicycle off the road and along the muddy edge of the field. Fortunately, the umbrella was stuck only a few feet in from the edge, so the traveler left his machine standing up, its wheels wedged deep enough in the mud to remain vertical. Then, delicately, he picked his way off the edge into the quaggy places en route to the umbrella. He looked about carefully, anxious to avoid insects and snakes. He didn't like snakes.

But a snake is just what he found: a big black cobra wrapped around the bamboo handle of the umbrella. So that's why the umbrella was upright! The traveler stopped, stood still, very afraid. Then the cobra spoke; as you might expect, the snake spoke English. The traveler, who had benefitted from a good education among the nuns of Saint Josaphat's Academy in Shiliguri, could speak English fairly well.

"I hope you were not thinking of stealing

my umbrella — it happens to be from a very fancy outfitter in Holborn."

"No, O Serpent of good family, I came only to observe this wonder, an umbrella open in an empty field, no person nearby. Excuse my intrusion."

"Am I not a person?"

"I meant no human person, your lordship."

"Ladyship. I am a female of the species."

"I'm sorry again, my Lady."

"I am not your lady. I am my lady."

"How clumsy I am, please excuse me again, I meant no insult."

"I believe you. You speak fairly well for a man from Bengal. Can you say 'snake'?"

"Shnake."

"I thought so. You found it odd that a poor serpent should shield herself from the heat or the sun and the pelting of the rain?"

"No, no, your Lady. I didn't see you, only the umbrella."

"You must understand that those of us who live flat on the ground all the time must take pains to avoid intemperate aggressions from the upper air — excessive heat and light and water and (I have been told) even ice and snow in the mountains. An umbrella is simple prudence. And naturally it is unfurled — what benefit a closed canopy?"

"I understand, now I know why the umbrella is here I will take my leave with thanks for the explanations."

"But what is that thing stuck in the ground over there?" said the snake, gesturing towards the upright bicycle. You must understand that there's only one way a snake can gesture, by pointing his head (in this case her head) at the thing intended. Her gesture now, towards the cycle, terrified the traveler, supposing it to be the first movement of a catastrophe. Luckily, though, he got the drift of her movement, which anyhow had stopped with the mere repointing of her glance.

"That is a bicycle, your Lady, it is mine, I have ridden it all the way from the Valley of the Teesta, and am on my way to Bodh Gaya, to pay my respects to Lord Buddha, a notable incarnation of Vishnu, we have been taught."

"Never mind that. How does it move?"

"I pump the pedals with my feet, and that makes the wheels turn, and as they turn, the machine moves ahead."

"Do not use that f-word around us. It is a painful word, redolent of the immense sacrifices our kind have made for your sake, so that we live in perfect contact with the wise earth, and can slip in and out of earth with ease, bringing wisdom and jewels and healing substances. Here, for you."

So saying, the cobra spat out a glittering amethyst. It trickled over to the traveler.

"May I pick it up?" he asked with fear.

"Certainly, it is yours now. It will help you remember the earth you roll across, and those who live on and in it. Perhaps someday it will help you to learn what we know."

Timidly, our traveler bent, slowly picked up the amethyst, and bowed deeply to the snake.

"Thank you, your Lady!"

The snake closed her eyes, lowered her head. It seemed like an acknowledgement of what he had said, so the traveler backed away towards his machine, tugged it out of the mud, kicked the spokes clear, dragged it back to the road, hopped on and went swiftly away. He cycled for a few moments before he realized he wasn't quite sure about which direction he'd been headed before he saw the umbrella.

In the Woods

HE WAS walking in the woods. It was the morning after his ninth birthday. Only one more year before he had two numbers to his age like all the grownups and the children he watched and followed and played with sometimes when he was bold.

It was a cold morning, misty, he thought how like water the mist is, drifting sluggishly through the trees.

He knew these woods pretty well, so he was surprised when he brushed past some dense bushes and came into a clearing and saw a picnic table sitting right there, and a man sitting at it, his back turned.

Edgar was a cautious boy, not exactly timid, but certainly cautious. He sidled along the edge of the clearing until he could see the man — heavy-set, not especially old, a bit grizzled. And the man was eating soup with a big spoon from a wooden bowl. Steam was coming off the bowl and stirring itself into the mist all round. And he could smell the soup.

Edgar wasn't especially hungry, but the soup smelled very good. He just stood there looking at the eater of soup.

Presently the man looked up. He had yellow eyes, very bright in his dull skin.

"Want some?" he said, sounding more like a fact than a question.

And all of a sudden Edgar did very much want some of that soup.

"Yes, sir, please, sir," he said, politely as he knew how,

The man pushed the bowl, still steaming, to the edge of the table nearest Edgar, and slid into it a long wooden spoon Edgar had not noticed before.

Edgar came slowly to the table, smiled at the man as if to say thank you, and picked the spoon out of the soup.

Instantly, as soon as his fingers touched the wood, his mouth filled with a rich excitement of tastes — he tasted roast pork and Christmas turkey, and baked salmon, and cheese pie his aunt made once a year, and cherries too, and hot pepper and sauerkraut and mashed potatoes, he tasted sausages and spaghetti and root beer and strawberry shortcake and raisins and steak. All the tastes at once battling in his mouth to see which was strongest, and they all were.

Edgar closed his eyes, frightened, he hadn't even tasted the soup but he had tasted it and everything.

He dropped the spoon, it fell back in the bowl and flicked up a drop of hot soup that landed on his wrist. He put his wrist to his mouth to lick the spot and when his tongue touched the drop of soup, all the tastes stopped.

He opened his eyes. No man. No table. Across the clearing a deer was looking at him, but when Edgar caught his glance, the deer turned and trotted away. The deer didn't even have yellow eyes.

Edgar was very hungry now, and hurried all the way home.

The Priest's Peculiar Wife

IN OUR parish a while ago there lived a young woman who fell in love with the curate at St. Botolph's, pursued him with mince pies and honey from her hives and watercolors she had made on her vacation in the Chablais. The young man was not hard to coax into similar feelings, and in a seemly season they were married. A few years later, the curate was presented to the living of St. Maude's in the next county, where he was installed as Vicar in his own right now, so we saw no more of him or of Fern, his wife.

Then, after a few years, we began to hear stories from those whose business took them over into that part of the world. It seems that our Fern had stopped presiding over the Ladies Guild, stopped attending the Parish Council meetings, and worst of all, had stopped entertaining at the Vicarage.

The vicar himself was seen to be plump and jolly and much as he had been, but his wife soon was hardly to be seen at all. Occasionally she'd be encountered walking quickly, in the gloaming of the evening or the day's first light, in some meadow or by the inconsequential stream they call a river in their vanity over there. In such encounters, the vicar's wife would acknowledge greetings and return them, eyes averted, and she would pass on without lingering to chat.

Soon the wits of the village began to pay close attention to the vicar's Sunday sermons and occasional feast day homilies. If he spoke of Hebrews and Philistines they were sure he was thinking of the baleful Delilah. If he spoke of Nazareth, they were certain he felt in his heart a grim contrast between the Holy Family and his own childless home and wildling wife.

For no child had come along to pin the girl down to her proper place. Speculation abounded. One officious person, a known troublemaker and frequenter of the public library, took it upon himself to write to the bishop, hinting and surmising and taking note with alarm. No answer came from the episcopal palace.

We in our town set to wondering. After all, she was one of ours, and her kin were all about us, each saner than the next, not a hint of night wandering. Should we do anything? A young man named Elphin (some parents just don't get the naming business) who had himself at one time been smitten with Fern decided to find out for himself. He was, I'm afraid, still keen on the girl.

Elphin saddled up and made his way to St. Maude's, and when he got there went boldly to the Vicarage. The aged housekeeper, a friendlier soul than most of her profession, received the young man courteously and installed him in the parlor. He waited.

After a bit the vicar came in, all smiles, and when he learned the object of Elphin's visit, explained that his lady wife was out on her charitable visits to the poor of the parish, but would surely be home within the quarter-hour, do wait. The vicar withdrew, and Elphin waited, comforting himself by communing with the cat asleep on the hearthrug.

Sure enough, in a few minutes Fern came rushing in, ruddy-cheeked, breathless, smiling to see him. She snatched his hand and dragged him to his feet.

"Come, we're going now. Why did it take you so long to come?"

Giving him no time to answer, she pulled him out the front door and down the path. At the road she unhitched his horse but instead of mounting it, slapped its haunch and sent it galloping away. Elphin watched aghast as his horse vanished towards the forest.

In that same direction Fern was tugging him now, "Come on, come on!" she kept urging. Soon she was running, and he had to run to keep up with her. Faster still, he did not know he could run so fast. Or that anyone could. In a few minutes they were moving so quickly he could barely feel the rocks and stubble they ran through. By now they had caught up his horse, and flashed past it.

Now they were in the trees, moved slower but still very fast. Time seemed to be running with them too, for Elphin was sure

it was still afternoon when he came to the Vicarage — it seemed to be full night now, and when they stumbled at last into a grassy clearing and stopped, a great white moon shone down on them. They stood there, Elphin gasping for breath, Fern perfectly still. Elphin heard crashing in the brush around him, and in a minute his horse, all lathered with sweat, came limping to join them.

Fern searched along the ground, found what she was looking for and snatched it up: a handful of thick grass, and brought it to the horse's mouth. Quickly he swallowed it, shivered, and stood still, at peace.

Fern took Elphin by the shoulders, looked at him seriously, said: "I am a little cross with you, you've made me wait so long."

What could Elphin say? No one, to his knowledge, had ever waited for him.

"But I forgive you," she went on, "we still have all the time in the world."

At once she stripped off her clothes and stood naked before him. But it was not the body he had perhaps guiltily imagined. It was a strong body, rough skin, and her hair seemed to move by itself. And as she turned this way and that, he was shocked to see a great curving lissome tail, long and thick as a tiger's, sprouted from the base of her spine. But before he could process this and seek in folklore for a name, let alone an explanation, she had in some savage gesture torn his clothes away. And his body too was not the one he knew or remembered. For one thing, it felt no weariness now, and for another it was covered with a fine soft fur, deep fur, as if he were a mink or a fisher. But he wasn't dreaming, she had slapped him hard, and at the slap he felt pain and knowledge all at once. But what was it he understood? Sometimes we feel we understand, understand, but can't put words to what we know.

Before he could do much thinking, Fern whistled, and out of the woods came bounding a creature like an ape, its dense matted hair all blonde and bronze, and only through the happy grinning face could Elphin recognize the Vicar of St. Maude's. Elphin feared the vengeance of a jealous husband, but he need not have done so. In his deep parsonical voice the vicar intoned, "Welcome, brother, we have waited for thee."

And they were off! Running this way and that through the trees, and then back out on the road, the horse running with them, all at the same pace, and the horse had sack after sack on its back, and from these the vicar and his wife, and eventually, as he grew more confident or just more carefree, Elphin too would take handfuls of food and medicine and even money, and toss it at the doorways of houses and cottages and shops and inns. And all that while they saw no one, though there were lights in all the windows, and here and there someone singing, or playing Mendelssohn on the piano.

And so it went, every night week after week, until the first snow came to ____shire, and the nightly donations had to stop. One morning Elphin woke up in the little bedroom they had made his in the vicarage and found the house empty, the fire burned out. He dressed quickly, shivering, and looked around. On the dining room table a note: *Dear Elphin. Thank you. Forever, F.*

Outside, he found his own horse all saddled and looking well-fed. He climbed on and the horse by himself took off for our parish. And here Elphin still lives, sad and grateful, unwed still, still pining for Fern, whatever she was or is, hair greying now, happier dreaming than awake, doing what he can to feed the poor and make the children happy, all that business of love we call charity, the kind of love we feel when the one we love is far from us but the love is real. Ask Elphin. Elphin knows. For I am he.

The Old Man and the Magpie

EVERYBODY knows that when you see a magpie first thing, you have to say "Good day, Sir!"

Well, there once was a somewhat somber old man who would rather say something rough than something pleasant, and would really rather say nothing at all. He wasn't exactly what children call mean, though there were some thoughtless people, and not just children, who called him a mean old man.

He was nice enough in his own way, though. He'd feed birds and squirrels if they happened to be near him when he was sitting in the park snacking, or feed ducks at pondside if he happened to have some bread in his pockets. And he often did, because deep down he was a kindly man, just a man who didn't have much use for talking with people, gossip, speculation, news. Whatever was going on around him was news enough for him, and whatever was going on in his head was conversation enough.

One day as the old man toddled out of his house and headed down the road towards the baker's, a magpie came hopping up the walk, all shining blue and black and white the way they do.

"Good day, Sir," said the man, more dutifully than with enthusiasm.

"Good day, yourself," said the magpie.

The old man was surprised, but not as much as you might think. He had always had the idea that birds, especially busy, noisy birds like crows and magpies and sparrows could talk if they wanted to.

"Good day indeed, Sir," said the man. "It's a pleasure to meet you."

"Not really meeting," said the bird, "since we've seen each other 1,674 times before today, and many of those times you greeted me, as is proper. Today I thought I should speak to you, since you look a little gloomy."

"No more than usual," said the man sadly.

"Exactly," said the magpie. "I thought it

was time to do something about it."

"What can you do?" The old man said this not in a disagreeable way, just simply as someone requesting information. And so the magpie understood it.

"Various things. Would you like to be young again?"

The old man thought about it, but not very long.

"No, I don't think so. I've been young already. In fact I was young for a long time, and didn't enjoy it all that much. I was always waiting for something to happen."

"Did anything happen?"

"I got older. I wouldn't want to go through that again."

The bird in his turn thought a while.

"Most old people want to be young again. I'm impressed that you don't. How about a nice wife, would you like one of those?"

"Ah," said the old man, "indeed I would. But wives die, you know, and then I'd be even sadder. Or I would die, and leave her in sorrow. Not good, these things."

The magpie pecked at its breast with its

beak a moment or two, then spoke again.

"You are indeed a thoughtful man. Maybe you can think of what would make you happier..."

"Why, yes," said the man, "I'll tell you. I just thought of it while we've been talking. I would like to understand the language of birds. It is my belief that birds always tell the truth, and say no more than they have to. They also sing a great deal, which cheers me. Do you think you could teach me the language of birds, at least to understand it? I probably couldn't learn to speak it, not at my age."

The magpie hopped up onto the man's shoulder, which startled the old man. It had been a long time since anyone was that close. But the old man was brave, and didn't flinch or shrug the bird away.

The magpie was whispering something into his ear.

"That's my deaf ear," the man said.

"Sorry," said the bird, and fluttered to the other shoulder. As it passed the man's face, the wing feathers brushed across the man's mouth.

Now the bird set to whispering again into the good ear. He began by reminding the man that for the past few minutes he had been conversing with a bird, not just understanding but speaking too.

"You have to start with one bird," the magpie went on, "then slowly you'll get to know others. Other magpies, first, then crows — who really are, I hate to admit it, the best speakers of all — then cardinals, blue jays, sparrows and so on. In this very life you'll be able to speak with hawks and falcons, though personally I never trust those birds, so be careful."

"But how will I learn?"

"You're already learning. Greet each one, the duck in the pond, the robin on the lawn, and listen to what they say, and say whatever's on your mind and listen to what they answer. Just listen. Just listen. Just listen."

And with that, the magpie flew up, circled the man and flew away.

The old man stood for a long time, right in that place, just trying to listen. He heard some finches yattering under a tree, and the steps of a dog trotting by, and a pigeon strutting fatly, cooing a little. And when a young courting couple happened along, he could even hear them too, the words they were saying to one another. He listened and listened and began to understand.

The Cat and the Butterfly

ONCE upon a summer afternoon a child was sitting on the grass of her parents' house (though she thought of it as her grass) and looking at a butterfly, sulfur yellow, flipping and dipping and skipping around the flowers. So many kinds of flowers. And even flowers that are the same kind are so different from one another. She sighed. How can you know all the names? How can you tell them apart? They're as bad as people. Her Aunt Esther and her Uncle Thad are always together but they looked completely different. How can they be the same kind of thing? And she and her stupid brother Evan, no resemblance at all. How can she expect two irises to look alike? She liked that flower, so soft and at ease and quiet, and she loved the name, it had her own name for herself in it, I-, and that made it special.

While she was pondering these things, the butterfly, and sometimes more than one of him, kept adventuring in the flowers. And the girl wasn't the only spectator. The family cat (her cat, when she remembered to feed it) Gatto was watching the butterflies too, occasionally looking away from them to the little girl.

"Do you know what I'm doing?" the cat asked.

The girl wasn't too surprised. If her Aunt Miriam, the one with red hair and no uncle to go with her, could drink wine and dance on the table once, just once, anything could happen once. So why not the cat? It probably has a lot to say.

"No, Gatto, I don't know. What are you doing?"

"I'm flying the butterflies around to amuse you. You do like them, don't you?"

"Yes, I do, I really do. But don't they fly by themselves?" She thought that was the whole point of being a butterfly, to look like fresh butter and fly around.

"No," said the cat, "that is a common

mistake, no doubt produced by the silly English name — in German and French we don't make the mistake of thinking butterflies fly — Schmetterling! Papillon!"

"What are you talking about, cat?"

"Sorry, I was speaking a grade or two above your level. To put it simply: butterflies do not fly. They are flown. And we are the ones who fly them."

"You mean you and I we?"

"No, dear child, we cats. Cats stay indoors all winter long, hence no butterflies. But lots of flickering shadows from candles and Christmas trees and such. In winter we cats fly shadows around the house, to keep in practice."

"Why can't I fly butterflies if I want to?"

"Why indeed. No reason that I know. Not being myself a human, I have only a vague idea of what humans can or can't fly or otherwise control. If you can fly butterflies, you'd know it. Just try for a while — it takes (he said modestly) a certain amount of practice, a certain skill."

"Maybe I can do other things," she said a

little peevishly, "maybe things you can't do."

The cat was peaceable with that.

"Very likely you can. What have you tried?"

The girl thought a moment, then a moment more, looking furtively this way and that around the garden.

Then she spoke boldly.

"I can make a stone stand still!"

The cat seemed impressed.

"That is a very great gift, and of great use to us all. It makes our squadrons of butterflies look rather petty, if pretty. Think how horrible it would be if stones were moving around all the time, leaping through the air, skipping out from under you, and from under buildings and banks and cathedrals! Life would be awful if rocks could run around at will. Bless you, dear child. You have a great skill, and I would envy you if animals knew envy. But we just know the word, but can't feel what it means."

Then Gatto looked away, and went on flying butterflies around the irises.

The Three Latin Scholars

ONE TIME in a town long ago and in a country where nobody spoke English, there were three little boys who were just beginning to learn Latin. That is the language they had been hearing in the church all their short lives, but now they had to learn it so they could grow up and be wise merchants or lawyers or councilors. No way to be wise if you don't know Latin, everybody knew that.

The old priest who was teaching them had begun by explaining that in Latin, the verb (the word that means doing something) had a different sound depending on who was doing it. Amo deum, I love God, Amas deum, you love god. Deus amat nos. God loves us. He explained it that way. And since he was a silly old priest, and there were three little boys, he nicknamed them Amo, and Amas, and Amat.

I love. You love. He, she, or it loves.

Little by little the boys started calling each other by these names too, just out of respect for the priest, and to practice their new language. When they were playing in the street, they'd call each other. Once it happened that Amas cried out, "Hey, Amat, Amat..." trying to get the third boy's attention to a wounded sparrow he had just found and wanted advice on caring for. Just as he cried Amat, Amat! a young man was passing, with his mind full of his girlfriend (her name was that of a flower we don't have here). The young man heard the cry and blushed, terribly embarrassed, thinking the boy was mocking him: He loves, he loves, he's in love with Gillyflower!

How did the boy know? Had his secret been discovered? Or did this boy have some magical power, to read the mind of a passerby?

The young man decided he had to know. So, being brave as a young man should be (and brave as Gillyflower would want him to be), he called to the boy.

"What's your name, sonny?" he said in

what he hoped was a pleasant way.

"Amas," the boy answered, looking at him with frank and open face.

The young man was startled. Because he understood the boy's name as saying "You love." And understood it as if it meant: You're in love, and I know it, and I'll tell the world.

The young man handed the boy an apple he'd been saving for elevenses, and hurried away, convinced that magic was in the air.

When he went to confession that Saturday afternoon, so he could be clean and fresh for taking the Sacrament the next morning, he eased his mind by telling the priest the story of the strange boy. As it happened, the priest was not the same one who taught the boys, or nothing more would come of this story. But the priest was young and earnest, and naturally feared the work of the Devil, well known to be active in towns of any size. He tried to ease the young man, warned him against excessive thinking about his girlfriend, or indeed about anyone but the Lord and His saints. And urged him to keep an eye on the boy, warily. "I am not sure," said the priest, "that you should have offered an apple to him – he might be a limb of Satan." The young man shuddered, and went away.

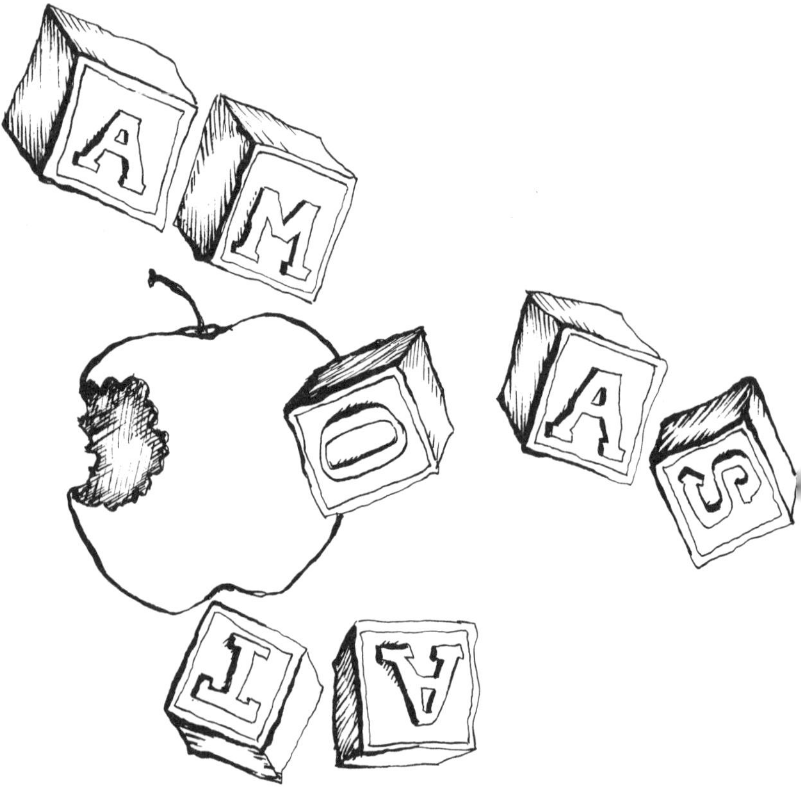

Meantime, Amas had taken the apple, had a bite, called his friends again. This time they came at his call, and studied the wounded bird. They all had bites of the apple, and pried off little chunks of soft flesh they brought to the bird's beak. He actually ate a few nibbles. Amo, who was good with his hands, gently carried the bird back to Amat's house, the nearest, and nestled him in a little box near the fire, to keep him warm. And sure enough, whether it was the apple or the warmth or the care, the bird took to fluttering, and soon enough flew out the kitchen door and away to his business.

While the boys were doing all this, the young earnest priest was writing to the bishop, telling him of the devilish child who knew the secret thoughts of a decent parishioner. When the bishop got the letter he was not much troubled. He was an old man, and had not had any trouble from Satan in many years, and was inclined to leave the Devil alone, hoping for the same in return. But to please the young priest he came the next Sunday to the church when all the people were gathered together. After the Mass and the singing, he had the beadles bring the boy to the front of the church. The boy asked his two friends to come with him and give him strength — they had no idea what was the matter.

The Bishop looked at the boy and said to him in Latin Who do you think I am? The boy, shaky in his Latin, answered with the one word he was sure of, his name. Amas, he said. And the bishop, who indeed was a loving and gentle person as bishops go, was amazed at the child's honesty. He called to another boy and asked in Latin, Can you tell us what God does? Amat, the child answered, his surest word. He loves us indeed, cried the bishop. And you young sir, he said to the boy who had been silent all this while, What do you say to God? Amo, said the boy, taking a cue from his friends. Ah, you love the Lord. That is well.

And with that, from a gold thing in his hand, he sprinkled holy water on the boys. Instantly the three schoolboys rose slowly into the air, and the people all gasped and then began singing a hymn, I forget which one, there are so many, as the boys floated above the congregation. Slowly they floated down the nave and out the great doors of the church into the sunlight, while the bishop and priests marveled aloud.

The next morning the good little boys went to the old priest for their lessons, to begin learning their next verb.

The Girl in the Curtains

EVERY day on his way home from school Joseph would pass a building all by itself on a block with vacant lots all round it. The building was one common in the early 20th century, three floors of apartments above a ground floor with two stores, an entrance door between them giving access to the stairs. The store on the left sold shoes, the store on the right sold toys. Joseph was too old for most toys now, so he seldom looked in the windows.

All the more so because of what he could see from across the street — that was his natural path home anyhow, and he usually stayed on that sidewalk, walking past the garage and the coal merchant and the bookshop, but keeping a close eye on that building all by itself on the other side of the street.

Because of the curious fact that almost every single day as Joseph passed it at 3:10 on his way home from school, he would see in the window just above the T of Toyshop a girl behind the glass. No sooner did she notice him gazing up at her than she would whisk closed the curtain by which, half-concealed, she was always standing. She looked like a pretty girl.

This had been happening for years now, almost every school day, the glance, his fascinated gaze, the abrupt vanishing. Joseph wondered if she did that to every passerby or just to him. Joseph wondered too whether she stood there at the window all afternoon every day, or just on school days.

So he made it his business one Sunday afternoon, when everybody was sleeping off the enormous Sunday dinners of those days, to creep back, coming from the home direction not the school, and wearing a big overcoat of his Uncle Hans, with a cap pulled down over his eyes. Sure enough, the girl was there. This time, she was looking in his direction, and as soon as she saw him peering up at her from across the street, she fluffed the curtain out in front of her. But it did seem to Joseph that there had been a second or two of hesitation, as if the act of recognizing him in his disguise took conscious attention.

So it went on, from fifth grade to sixth to seventh, to eighth and finally now, eleventh grade, and Joseph a fine young adolescent getting ready for the world. And also getting ready to play the man, to address th world of women. This woman.

One Friday in November he could stand it no longer. As he shivered in the drizzle he looked up at her, and at once the cloth came between them. But this time he darted across the street and tried the entrance door. It opened at a touch. He hurried up the stairs before his resolution wavered, and pounded on the door of the apartment, first floor front, that must give entrance to the room where the girl stood.

The door swung open as if from the mere force of his knocking. Joseph stepped in, and heard the door close behind him. It was very bright in there.

As his eyes got used to the glare, he saw that the room, if it was a room, was very big. It stretched away into the distance, full of sun and sand. It looked like a desert, like a film he had seen once of the Arabian desert, just sand and yellows and shadows that seemed almost solid chunks of darkness, under a sky hot blue as a welding spark. At his feet he saw sand, clearly sand. There was no sign of the girl or her curtain or the window she stands at, stood at so many days, so many years. Just more desert, with a rise of mountain in the far distance. He was thirsty. He was afraid.

Behind him, where the door had been, a growling sound. He spun round and saw a fat little old man sitting cross-legged in sand, and making noises like a dog. Or a lion.

"You have come for my daughter at last," the man said.

"I came to see her, I have seen her for so many years, I wanted to know her, forgive me, I shouldn't have just come in like this. But I wanted to see her, really see her, and ask her why she always hides from me behind the curtain." Joseph surprised himself by saying so much, and so clearly, and by saying what he really meant.

"No," the old man said, "there is no curtain. I think it must be something in you, in your eyes. Maybe you have ..." He paused, as if seeking some technical term, for an ophthalmic condition, "...maybe you have shy eyes."

Joseph didn't know what to say. Maybe the man was right. But even so, where is the girl?

"Where is she, though, your daughter."

The old man laughed. "Oh you, you really do have shy eyes. She's right here, just look round you. She is the sunlight on the sand, the blue in the sky, the heat in the sand around your feet. She is everything you can see. Everything wants to show itself to you, yet people are afraid to see, their eyes are shy, or lazy, or afraid. For years you have not let yourself really see what you see. Now go to sleep a while. She'll come and tuck you in."

Joseph was overwhelmed with torpor and sank down into the nice soft warm sand. He felt someone's fragrant breath on his cheeks, on his mouth, and then he slept.

When he woke up, he was standing out in the street, facing his home. He walked mechanically in the right direction, thinking, or trying to think. He did not think he would ever see the girl again. But who knows?

A Puzzled King

THE KING was puzzled. In the very same week two ambassadors had reached his court. One came from Ostrova, the wild land to the east of his kingdom. The other came from Galtorna, the heavily wooded kingdom to the west. Each ambassador had in essence the same mission. To offer to the king the hand of the princess of his country, Olya of Ostrova, Berid of Galtorna, each the daughter of the reigning sovereign.

Each ambassador had brought a painted image of his princess, Olya's pale face and high cheekbones rendered prettily in a gold oval frame, Berid's darker, enigmatic beauty painted on a metal plate.

It wasn't clear whether the ambassadors knew of one another's mission. But the king knew, and for once in his decisive life, didn't know what to do.

So he summoned his wise men to a late night session in his securest tower chamber. They brought their tools with them, astrological, magical mathematical. He laid the problem before them, showed them the painted images of his bride-to-be. Which one should he choose?

Wizard Waldo and Wizard Wolfo got to work, The king grew sleepy watching them fussing with charts and diagrams, whirling tops, calculations on the abacus with the beads flying back and forth.

A discreet cough snapped the king out of his doze.

"Majesty," said Wizard Wolfo," we have consulted stars and planets, numbers and names, words and shadows. We have summoned certain angels known to me (though not to Waldo), and others he claims exclusive rights to call. "

Waldo interrupted: "All my claims are true!"

Wolfo smiled, as at a child, and went on. "In the final analysis, your Majesty, the truth of the matter is that we could not decide. It's not so simple as to say that Waldo chose Olya and I chose Berid, not so, and not the other way round. Both ladies seem admirable, for beauty and for their essentic burden."

The king didn't know what that phrase meant, and said so.

"It means, your Majesty," said Waldo this time, "the whole weight of past lives and their consequences in this life. As Plato reports in the last book of his Polity, such a burden plays a great role in one's present life."

Plato indeed. The king had not stayed up well past midnight to hear bearded loons dither about some Greek.

"Which woman should I choose?" he asked, abruptly.

The two wizards spoke for once in unison: "We really can't be sure, Your Majesty. Each lady is worthy, virtuous and kind. Each is likely fertile with princes of the blood to come. They seem equal in our view."

The king dismissed them, rather curtly, and made his way to bed, hoping sleep, that most ancient of all wizards, would make his choice clear in the night.

But the king woke uninstructed. Irritated, puzzled, half-inclined to toss a coin and be done with it. After his servants had dressed him and he had drunk a goblet of pomegranate juice from far off Halicia mixed with water, he went down and wandered in his private garden.

He stood looking at the marble fountain, oldest fountain in the whole castle. It burbled feebly these days, a cheery sound though, and its waters clear and sweet. As he watched the water tumble up and fall and its ripples spread, he tried to find a handle to his problem. There was no easy political solution — both countries were long-time allies of his own realm, and he had no reason to suspect that choosing one princess would make trouble with the land of the other, rejected royal.

And then a crow fluttered down and perched on the edge of the fountain — not a usual place for crows, the king knew. The king stared reverently at the crow (as it is always correct to do) and said out loud, "What should I do, O Crow?"

"Come with me and you will see," said the crow in its calm sharp voice, and leapt into the air.

Instantly the king rose up too, was flying, no, floating fast, effortless high into the sky above his tower, his castle, his whole city spread out below him, wider and wider, the central province, the shires spreading out to the edges of the kingdom, higher and higher rose the king until he was at the top of the sky, and could see the evening shadows creeping in the east over Ostrova, and the blazing midday sunshine of Galtorna, his whole world.

And still the crow was above him, fluttering "What do you see, what do you see?" the crow kept asking. The king started listing all the things he could see, rivers and mountains, glaciers, cathedrals, ships on the sea, a fire burning in the hills, a storm flashing and thundering three hundred miles away.

"Not those, not those!" cried the crow. "Look and see the face of the one you need, the one who needs you, the one you will marry."

The king looked east and saw no sign of Olya, looked west and no Berid to be seen. Then he looked down, straight down, and there, far, far beneath him but suddenly clearly seen, a woman walking along a street in his own city, a woman with red hair, who moved swiftly between stone houses.

The king began to sink, quickly, but with no feeling of dizziness or dread. Down he sank until he was close to the streets below, and could watch the woman, and finally, as she turned to mount the stone steps of a chapel. see her face,

"This is she," the crow remarked quietly, and flew away.

And suddenly the king was back in his garden. And he knew what he had to do. In a few hours his courtiers had found and identified the woman, daughter of a local jeweler, grand-daughter though of a traveler from the far north who had practiced medicine in the city for many years.

The girl was brought to the king's throne room and introduced to the monarch, who told her as simply as he could that she was his chosen, his bride, his beloved. She accepted all this calmly, and with grace.

As news of the royal betrothal spread, the visiting ambassadors accepted the decision and made their departure, each secretly glad that the other princess had been rejected. And after all, why shouldn't the king choose to marry one of his own countrywomen? That seems only natural when you think about it.

The Wind and the Wolf

ONE NIGHT the wind was howling and a wolf looked up. Are you talking to me?, asked the wolf. The wind howled some more. You are talking to me, I can tell, but I'm not sure what you're saying. The wind howled even louder so the wolf howled back. The wind howled more, and the wolf understood.

It is cold tonight, so cold. You make me colder, colder even than the winter and the dark, but my fur keeps me warm, or warm enough. And the wolf curled up into a snug bundle under the low snow-heavy branches of the spruce.

Then the wind really began to howl, louder and louder and at a high pitch that almost hurt the wolf's sensitive ears. The wolf covered his ears with his paws, but the wind went on.

Suddenly the wolf understood what the wind was saying.

You are cold but you have fur, the wind says. I am running through this cold world, says the wind. I am running so fast but I have no fur and no coat and no paws to cover my lips, I howl with cold and there is no one to warm me, says the wind. I howl with cold, I hope I wake somebody up who will warm me, I hope I wake everybody up and maybe all their breaths together will warm me.

Only time will really warm you, said the wolf, but I'll try. And the wolf got to his feet and faced into the wind, and opened his big mouth and breathed out a low, long hot howl, quivering his hot red tongue to make the howl warble and trill, and his breath was hot with the blood of all the animals he had from hunger been forced to kill and eat, hot with his own hot blood and anger and fear, because a wolf has great fear, and out he breathed it all into the wind, the face of the wind.

The wind felt it, and sank low for a moment, sighed a little with relief. Thank you, said the wind to the wolf. Now both the wind and the wolf were a little less cold now, felt the same relief. The wind said thank you again, and the wolf said that too.

And the wind said I never knew that wolves could be afraid.

The wolf answered, Fear makes language, fear makes us speak. Everything that speaks knows how to be afraid.

Shadow Talk

I WONDER what my shadow would say if it could talk," the boy wondered. He was sitting on the floor in the parlor, a nice thick Axminster carpet from Wanamaker's soft beneath him. And under it there was a special matting his mother had explained. It protects the rug and the floor and the feet and everything. Jute.

He was watching his shadow, half of it on the sideboard, half askew on the pale wall beside it. The part on the sideboard, right under the cut-glass bowl full of oranges, was the shadow of his left shoulder, the wall part his right shoulder. I am both places at once, he thought. A strong light was coming from behind him, the setting sun shining through the picture window.

But if the shadow could talk it would be another person, wouldn't it, so the part on

the sideboard would be the shadow's right arm, and the wall part his left. My right his left, just like a mirror, he thought. And sure enough, when he raised his left arm, the shadow raised its right arm.

This is confusing. A shadow is all black, no mouth, no eyes, and a reflection in a mirror has all the parts that I have. But somehow they're both me. But my left his right.

"Her right," the shadow said.

The boy wasn't sure but he thought he'd heard the shadow speak, a high mellow gentle voice, sounded like her right, or hurry out or something like that. Though the shadow has no mouth, so how can it speak? The boy decided to try an experiment.

"Hello, shadow," he called, loud. He reasoned that it might be an echo, after all, an echo is like the shadow of a sound.

"What do you want?" the shadow said.

This was clearly no echo.

"Are you really my shadow?"

"Whose else could I be — do you see anyone else in the room? We are alone. You are my Opacity, I am your shadow."

"What's an opacity?" Curiosity overcame his sense of strangeness in talking to the wall. Or the sideboard. Where was the mouth anyway?

"You are an Opacity, my special one. An Opacity is anything that blocks the light. By doing so, it forces the light to shape itself around the Opacity, leaving a more or less accurate image of the Opacity on any surface otherwise brightened by the light. This Image is a Shadow. I am one. You are my Opacity. You belong to me."

"But you're my shadow! So you belong to me."

"That also is true. We belong to you, but it's hard for you to control us. We're always changing, according to the light, the dark, the movements of our Opacities. For example, right now I have no legs because you're sitting on the floor with your knees drawn up to your chin, chatting with me. So I have no feet, no legs, no hands, no arms — your arms are wrapped round your knees. How inert I am, I'm like the shadow of a mountain, not a man. I mean a boy. But I have a head still, so I can talk to you."

"Why don't you sound like me, if you're my shadow?"

"Well, I'm much more learned than you, I've been around a lot, and you've made me mingle with the shadows of other people — your mother, your father, your friends at school — and when shadows mingle on a wall, when one shadow mingles with someone else's shadow, each shadow automatically knows everything the other shadows know. Shadows are of one substance, one flesh, all alike. It's automatic."

"That's scary, you know everything my father's shadow knows?"

"Yes, and your uncle's, and the priest who christened you, and the teacher who shook your hand when you graduated from kindergarten, and the mailman you talked to one day on the sidewalk, when he was all sweaty from the bright sun. All of them."

"But why doesn't your voice sound the least little bit like my voice?"

"Because a shadow is always the gender opposite her Opacity. I am what you would call a Girl Shadow, and will eventually be a

Woman Shadow as you get older — but there won't be any difference in me, only in you. I will follow your movements faithfully, and I'll try to understand why you do the things you do, silly things, stupid things, smart things. And when you grow up a little, you'll be able to ask me questions, and I will answer out of the great store of my knowing, and then you'll know some of what I know. You'll say Shadow, Shadow on the wall, how shall I make my true love call? And I will answer, Just stare at the wall and remember!"

"But I don't have a true love."

"That was just an example. You will have loves soon enough, true and otherwise. Be careful to ask me which is the true one. Meantime, always stare at the wall and remember."

Taking Turns

MILLIE and Sarah were more than best friends. They were best friends, indeed, but they were also more like sisters. Like friends they could run around and play and have fun and make things together, but like sisters they could fight and snarl and snap at each other but soon make up.

They had been together since third grade when Millie had moved into the neighborhood. Now six years later they were still close — even closer, in fact, trying on each other's clothes and discussing this new phenomenon of boys being interesting, sharing secrets, all the usual things.

Then one Monday morning Sarah wasn't in class, didn't show up the whole day. Millie even called her a few times and texted but no answer. Millie felt that mixture we always feel when a friend isn't responding — first annoyance at friend's silence, slowly blending with anxiety about friend's well-being.

Millie walked the few blocks to Sarah's apartment house, rang the buzzer a few times but no answer, and the main door stayed locked. So Millie went home, grumpy a bit. And when her mother called out cheerily "No Sarah today?" (because they played together or I guess at their age we should say they hung out together) every afternoon, Millie only grunted, went to her room and read a book for a while.

But there's only so much a book can do for you, when you're hungry or miss a friend. As she stared at the ceiling, the phone rang in the other room — the landline, which they seldom bothered to answer, all spam, and surveys. Not this time, her mother picked up the phone right away. Millie could hear a longish conversation going on, or just her mother's voice brief in long silences. Millie wondered what was going on.

A few minutes passed, and her mother came in without knocking, sat down on the edge of the bed, her face pale, almost frightened.

"What is it, mom, what's the matter?" Her mother took a deep breath and looked at her, tears in her eyes.

"It's your friend, dear little Sarah. She's been in an accident, her family, the car. She's dead, darling, she's dead. The whole family died in the crash."

Then her mother took her in her arms and hugged her close, crying. Millie was not crying, though, she didn't know what to feel, she felt nothing, just the word dead, dead, kept sounding in her mind. What does it mean? What will I do?

Slowly she began to feel her way to her mother's feelings; she knew her mother was crying for her, not for herself. Millie tried to share the grief, and little by little the tears came.

After a while, they both stopped crying. Her mother gently toppled Millie onto the bed, covered her with a quilt, kissed her brow and went away. She left the light on.

Finally, as Millie lay there, she began to feel angry. She threw off the coverlet and sat up in bed, breathing hard. Sarah had left her, left her alone, abandoned her for this death thing. She got mad enough to speak, and almost snarled, "Sarah, where are you? I need you!"

As soon as the words were out of her mouth, Sarah walked out of the closet, the door didn't open, Sarah just appeared through it, stood in front of Millie.

"Here I am. I'm sorry you're angry and sad, I couldn't help it. I didn't mean to leave you, I just died."

Millie leapt up and tried to hug her with joy and relief, but her arms felt nothing, just passed through Sarah the way Sarah had passed through the door.

"I can't feel you!"

"But I felt you," Sarah said, "it was like a warm fresh breeze passing through me, your arms."

Millie wanted to know what else Sarah felt, could she feel the door she went through, could she taste things? What was it like being dead?

Sarah said "I don't know much about being dead yet, they haven't told me anything,

I'm just trying to pick things up as I go along. Would you like to feel what it's like for yourself? I think we can do that."

"Do what?" Millie asked.

"We can take turns being dead."

Before Millie had a chance to think about it or get frightened at the idea, Sarah had come forward and settled down into Millie, and Millie found herself, or not herself, just her mind, across the room where Sarah had been standing, and on the bed she saw her own body sitting firm on the mattress, and Sarah looking at her out of Millie's eyes.

Millie ran her fingers down her body and felt only the ripple of air, reached out for a stuffed bunny she's had since childhood, her fingers passed right through the fur and the cotton stuffing, and the rabbit didn't move an inch.

It was so exciting that she forgot to be scared. And meanwhile the Millie on the bed was touching and squeezing everything in sight, getting back to the physical world, her face full of a delight that real Millie had never seen.

"How did you do that?" Millie asked.

"I just walked into you, and became you. You can do it now too."

So Millie-in-Sarah walked over, tentatively, and pounced down into Millie-on-the-bed, and she was herself again, and there was Sarah standing by the closet door again.

"Did you like that?" Sarah asked.

"I think I did."

"Well I liked it too. We can do that any time we want, because we love each other and tell each other the truth, don't we?"

Millie jumped up to embrace Sarah lovingly, and this time she became Sarah and Sarah became Millie and it happened so fast over and over that both girls felt embraced and complete.

So for a long while that afternoon they sat and made their plans. They decided that Sarah would be dead in the daytime, so Millie could go on being in school and planning for college, the Millie could be dead at night, when no one would expect much of her. They agreed to try this for a month.

Now Millie that very night found out

some of the wonderful things the dead can do. They can go anywhere and be anywhere on earth just by thinking about it, can watch the world and hear it, sometimes even get a whiff of perfume or the odor of roasted meat, sometimes even dare to get close, close to people, sometimes so close that the people shivered a little without knowing why, or even felt a little tenderness for no reason they could say.

Sometimes she would follow her own body around as Sarah slipped out of the apartment while Millie's mother was sound asleep, and Sarah would go clubbing or dancing Millie's body around town, having fun. Once Millie even saw Sarah get a kiss from a boy who'd always been after Millie and that Millie didn't much like — but there he was, pecking Millie's lips. Millie found it hilarious.

Millie traveled to Paris right away, then Sri Lanka and Thailand and New Zealand where she watched an uncle she'd heard of but never met had a sheep farm. She went to Athens, and when she was there she realized that she could go back in time to other time-spots. And even go to places that didn't exist on earth, but that she'd read about or seen in movies. But she liked the real places best, Norway was great, she didn't feel the cold at all, and the Himalayas, and the temples of north India.

Her daytimes were pretty dull — and she was sleepy a lot of the time, her mind so busy all night long. If it had gone on much longer, her grades would have suffered and people would be talking about depression and doctors.

But the month was soon up. Sarah and Millie had arranged to meet in a park at noontime, when Millie would be in her own body and Sarah at the peak of her presence (as she described it).

Millie could tell right away that something was wrong, Sarah looked so sad.

"What is it, Sarah, what's the matter?"

Sarah sat down or seemed to, on the park bench beside her.

"Our month is over, and I don't think we can have another. I've loved being you, I love you more than ever. But I have to go away

now. They told me it's time for me to go on. I don't know what that means, or where I'm going, but they're very clear, and very strict."

"But who are they?" Millie wanted to know.

"I don't know who they are, they're just

voices and presences that tell me this and that. They seem kind but stern, like schoolteachers. And just this morning they told me that I have to say goodbye to you and this area of time and go on. They stressed go on as if I knew what it meant. But they didn't say. So now I have to say good-bye, dear friend. I hope you've enjoyed being dead as much as I enjoyed being you for a while. Maybe you can still keep doing in your mind what you were able to do in my old body. You'll find out, and I'll find out what it means to go on."

And Millie reached out to hug Sarah one last time, but already there was no one there, and Millie almost toppled off the bench, but pulled up just in time.

The Carpet

HIS MOTHER died when he was five and within a couple of years his father had married again. The new wife was a perfectly nice woman, not mean or neglectful, who treated him kindly, maybe even as if he were her own. But little by little, all traces of his real mother vanished from the house — her clothes, of course, even her lovely old seal fur coat, the breakfast china, the bedroom dresser and chifferobe all new. The only thing left from his mother's sway was the big old Oriental rug in the dining room, under the seldom-used table and his eight chairs.

The rug probably would have gone away too, except that it seemed to be valuable, somehow, and the new wife liked it. She called it an Isfahan — he didn't know what that meant and was, but he really liked the rug, and was glad it stayed.

Whenever he felt lonely or sad, which was pretty often, and missing his mama, he'd get down and curl up on the rug. His father and step-mother thought this was cute, and imagined with amusement that he was under the dining room table, pretending it was a cave or a temple or a little fort, the way kids do.

He let them think that. But he was really there to be with his mother. He'd lie on that big soft dusty plain, all red and blue and golden scrolls and leaves and curlicues on a field of sand, study the pattern, follow the lines of color with his finger tips, rest sometimes his cheek on the sandy background or bursts of color, close his eyes and remember mother.

And one afternoon, when they were out at shopping, it must have been a Saturday, he was alone in the house and more lonely than usual. He lay down on his carpet, her carpet, and watched the motionless movement of the colored scrollwork and intricate designs right in front of his face. Suddenly the leaves and twists began to move, writhe round, straighten out or curve more. As we watched, they began to form letters, write words.

He had learned to read long ago, at least a year now he'd been reading his books and even a book or two from the public library only six blocks away. So he had no trouble reading what the rug was saying.

My dear Son, I will always be with you, the carpet wrote, and he began to cry, which made it harder for him to read the next words that came along. Don't be too sad, a little sadness is good, it tells me you miss me. But I love you very much, and it makes me very, very sad to see you sad. I will always be close to you, never fear.

When he had read all that in the swirling pattern, he had stopped crying. He felt even a kind of new secret, a secret sorrow that felt a little like joy.

And over the next few years he often lay there, languid it seemed, while his elders chuckled at his play-fort, he'd lie there and read his mother's words. From her he learned many things, right there on the dining room floor, about time and space and weaving, and what colors mean, what to do about fear. Later still she guided him about the qualities to look for in a friend, and in turn how to be a good friend to people, and a good son, even to that new woman who lived with his father and made him happy. All we should ever try to do is make one another happy — I will always be here for you, and being able to talk to you makes me happy too.

When it was time for household chores, he always insisted on being the one to vacuum the carpet, and this usually amused his parents, who'd say Look, he's cleaning his fort.

The Leper's Touch

ONCE upon a time, hundreds and hundreds of years ago, there lived a leper. Like many lepers he came from a good family and had been a sturdy, affluent young man when the disease came upon him. The demons who cause leprosy, like many other Morbiferous Demons, do not want to waste their spores or seeds on the feeble or the fated. No, they prefer the plump to the meager, the young to the old. Leprosy demons want to live a long, relaxed life in their host, without much bothering to move from victim to victim.

So our leper had been robust as you please when the tell-tale bronze patches appeared, the white scurf, the odd failure of sensation here and there. His family was certainly supportive and capable of providing him with a secluded cottage to which his needments would be brought by cautious though respectful servants.

Our leper, though, was of a melancholy bent (for Saturn is the lord of affliction and reflection both), and considered carefully what he ought to do. The conclusion to which he came was this: that he would embrace this terrible obstacle and take it somehow as a path. In his country at that time most lepers wandered around alone or in scruffy bands begging for provender. So he fitted himself out with warm clothes and set out on his life of exile. His weeping parents presented him with a little silver bell to ring, to warn strangers of his condition as he approached them, as the law required. He turned and smiling through his own tears rang the little bell at them and set off.

You can imagine his life for the next few years, wandering, being shunned, being helped, being fed, going hungry, freezing, sweltering. We still live in the same world, nothing has changed, you know as well as I do what it felt like to go day after day in all seasons on this planet. Where to sleep.

Where to bathe. Where to void. Enough said.

Five long years our leper wandered through his country, occasionally drifting across the borders of other princedoms, never going far, though, from those whose language was his own.

One pleasant spring day, really the first warm day of the year, he stopped and carefully wiped the sweat from the sores on his face, then bent to drink from a clear stream, just a rill, running alongside the road. As he drew near the water, he was shocked to see how ugly and deformed he had become. It felt very strange to gulp the water then, as if he were drinking ugliness, accepting his own ruination. I accept what I am given, he thought, may all be well.

Later that day he came into a town, always ringing his silver bell (the envy of all the lepers, and a few little children too young to know anything but the bright silver, the sound). People drew away from him, naturally. But there, on the ground, a man lay groaning. At first the leper thought the man was drunk already and not even midday yet. But then he heard him cry for help and groan, and cry again. As his eyes caught sight of the leper, he called, please, you, please, help me.

It had been a long time since anyone had asked the leper for anything — a leper's life is all receiving, it seems — so he was a little unsure of what to do. He rang his bell loud as he could and approached the man.

"Give me a hand," the man called, "I am sick, I can't get up."

Obediently the leper held out his healthier hand, the man took hold, the leper pulled with all his little strength and the man was able to rise.

"Thank you, sir. I feel much better now, much better indeed."

The color had come back into the man's face, and he looked ten years younger than he had a moment before. He smiled at the leper and walked away.

An old woman had been watching from a doorway, and now, clutching her chest, she boldly came towards the leper. He rang his bell and backed away, but she moved quickly.

"Touch me," she cried, "touch me here,"

she said, pointing her thumb at her chest. Timidly, the leper lifted his hand to her chest.

"The pain is gone!" she cried, grabbed the leper's hand, kissed it and hurried away, and was soon surrounded by people asking and judging. The leper was edging away, uneasy about the whole business, not knowing what to think. And a voice inside him seemed to say You don't need to think. Just carry on.

The leper paused by the church steps and a young mother came towards him, leading a pretty young child limping painfully, his left leg half-genuflecting at each step.

"Please!" the mother said.

The leper bent and touched the boy's leg, the boy gasped, crumpled to the ground, immediately jumped up and walked around, danced around laughing, no trace of a limp.

That morning the leper must have cured or eased the pain of twenty-seven people in the town. By evening he was sitting alone on the church steps, a few people watching him warily, reverently, fearfully, from across the little square.

At the ringing of the angelus, the air dark-

ening already, the leper got up and made his way out of town. When he bent to drink from the next stream he met (for lepers as you know are not allowed to drink from wells or fountains), he could hardly see his face in the swift water, but what he saw scared him a little — he looked much older, and the marks of his condition, the swollen cheeks of the lion mask (as they called it), much puffier, gashed. And his hands felt strange.

And so it went on for the next year or so, the leper becoming the healer of all, and every healing weakening him further. I accept what I am given and I give what I can, is how he thought about it. Obscurely he knew that the demons of his disease were not happy about him curing so many people — and even a sick horse once, and a moaning cow — so they were punishing him; yet didn't they realize they were ruining their own residence by doing so? Ah, sickness is a mystery, he thought, as big a mystery as birth and death.

By now his hands were like claws, he could barely hold his bell, and there was not much left of his nose. He thought maybe he should make his way to his home, maybe his family needed healing too. Why hadn't he thought of that before.

He set out homeward but never got there. He met so many crippled people and ailing folk along the way, he had to heal them all, had to touch each one, and at every touch there was less and less of him until one day when he bent down to drink he did not rise again.

The bishop of those parts consecrated a small plot of ground adjacent to the real churchyard, and men wearing handkerchiefs over their noses and mouths, handkerchiefs soaked in lavender and thyme, carried the dead leper to the place and buried him there, with much Latin spoken.

For a time, people would come to the grave hoping to be healed, and some of them were. There was even talk of declaring him a saint, but no one could remember his ever having practiced religion. And furthermore, nobody knew his name. You can't have a saint without a name.

The Crow Girl

ONCE upon a time on the side of the hill turned away from the rising sun there lived a girl who was very good to crows. Every morning she would come downstairs and carefully bring together all the scraps of food from the night before that she or her family — for they were frugal — had not managed to eat before they went to sleep. She would take the scraps outside and toss them on the snow or on the grass depending on the season, so that the crows could come and have their breakfast too. After her own breakfast, she always made sure to have three or four or five or six or sometimes more cookies or scraps of bread to bring out to her friends the crows.

Now as you know, crows understand a great deal. And they are very good to people in general, especially to people who are good to them. But whether you're good to crows or not, a crow is always looking out for your best interests. If you're walking in the woods at night or just before night, and you don't know which way to turn, listen for the crow. The crow will caw caw caw in the direction you're supposed to go. Just follow the crow. Well, crows are like that to everybody, but they're especially attentive to those who, like the girl on the side of the hill, take good care of the crows.

One morning, in a season of the year that was not full winter yet and had not been summer for a long time, fairly early the girl came downstairs to look around the kitchen and living room and the dining room (and those are the only rooms the house had downstairs) but she could find no scrap of food for her friends. She looked in the bread box and found a couple of stale pieces of bread — think if the crows were given just this sad bread. You wouldn't want to think about their disappointment. She took the two pieces of bread and stood by the fire and toasted them a little, then spread some honey on, and brought them outside and put them on the ground. They looked so pretty sitting there on the dew. Then she realized it would be hard work for a crow to pick up the big bread in its slim beak. So she bent down and broke up the toast into little bits that she arranged neatly and gently on the grass, They looked even prettier now, like stars. Then the girl licked the honey off her fingers as she went back towards the house, and as she finished licking the last finger clean (it was the ring finger on her left hand, it was), something happened in the back of her mind.

She seemed to sail up in the air, till she was high above the house, high above the trees, even above the hill. She was looking down on house and hill, floating easy, and she skimmed gently in the sky. It is cold up there so she shivered a little and the shivers ran down her arms and along her sides, and the shivers seemed to take on a life of their own. They were her feathers. They rippled and lifted her along, or she moved them, she wasn't certain which came first, the feather or the bird. I must be a bird, she thought, and looked about and saw that she was, and knew she could skim along the cloud and rise easily on the current of warm air coming up from the sunlight that had just begun to warm the other side of the hill. She could ride that current or just stand quietly in the sky and cry out to her friends. Caw, caw, she said, and the sound felt good coming out of her mouth.

But it is hungry work, she found, this flying business, especially on a brisk morning when you haven't had your breakfast. Down there she spotted the bits of bread and honey like stars on the grass, and swooped down to have a taste. But as she landed, she remembered that she had put them out for her friends the crows. But I'm a crow, she thought, opening her beak towards one of the morsels. But then she thought, I'm not those crows, my crows. This food is for them. Just then, two crows landed not far away, keeping their distance, the way they do, and looked at her.

You must be you, said one crow to her. Yes, I am, she said, and you're my friends. Come have some breakfast. We've eaten already, said the other crow, but a snack would be pleasant. With that, the two crows hopped over to the toast.

How big crows are! she suddenly realized, big as her whole self, these huge black friendly birds with such bright eyes. She watched them pick at the toast, then each picked up a morsel and flew off to a branch and watched her as they ate. Thank you, one crow said, and thank you, said the other.

She was very hungry now, and the toast looked very tempting. But it was for them, imagined, intended, given. So she thought she'd go into the house and see what else there might be to eat. She hopped across the lawn and up the old stone step and in at the kitchen door. No sooner was she in the house than she became a girl again. She looked back at the tree, the crows were watching. She wasn't sure she was glad or sad, being a girl again. She waved to the crows, and tried to call, but it sounded now a little more like barking. She laughed at herself, and tried again. The crows, both of them, cawed at her. Encouraging, it sounded. And she realized she could understand what they were saying, just as plain as speaking English. One crow said, See how easy it is? And the other crow said, Any time, any time.

The Sofa

PAUL'S house was tall and narrow, one of a long row of tall, narrow houses along one side of a street. Across the street there were only empty fields, so it was nice to look out the windows.

Downstairs was a bathroom and a kitchen and a dining room. Upstairs were his little bedroom, his parents' big bedroom, and in the front of the house a big living room. Hardly anyone ever used the living room.

When company came, they usually sat in the big kitchen or for more formal occasions the dining room. And that was where the uncles would come and play pinochle or even watch television, because that's where the big screen was. But only solemn occasions ever brought people to the living room, parties to celebrate weddings or births or birthdays.

But Paul used the living room a lot, and

he was permitted to do so. In fact, there was an older green armchair in one corner that had his name on it. It was a bit shaggy, but it even had a cushioned stool his mother called an ottoman — but didn't that mean a Turk?

So Paul was allowed to sit there as long as he liked. And he did like, a lot of light swept in from the big bay windows and fell on the books he loved to read, or at night too the sconces on brackets gave enough light to go on reading. Though he was not ever supposed to bring food into the living room, he would sometimes sneak a candy bar or a piece of fruit in to enjoy while reading. Once in a while his mother would find a scrap of orange peel in the green upholstery and fuss at Paul a while, but then get over it.

But there was one thing he was never allowed to do. Against the main wall stood, on carved legs, a stiff sofa, with red and silver stripes running down the back and out across the seat. The cushioned seat was stiff and not comfy at all, and the sofa sat high enough off the ground so it wasn't comfortable for a child to sit on — Paul could just perch there at best. But he was not allowed to.

It seems that this sofa was precious, made by some famous company and brought from France long ago, and had to be kept in perfect condition. No member of the family ever sat on it, but well-attired guests were invited to rest there during gatherings. Paul couldn't understand the whole business of the sofa, but knew he was never ever supposed to climb onto it.

Which, of course, he wanted to do, the way we always want to do what is forbidden. So one evening, when his parents were out at some meeting, Paul closed his storybook, tucked it down between the cushion and the arm of his green chair, got up and walked across the living room, stood staring at the sofa.

He stood there a few minutes. He had to know what it was like to sit on that thing. Maybe even lie on it — it was plenty long enough for that. Finally he kicked off his shoes to avoid leaving any traces, and calmly climbed onto the sofa and stretched out.

Instantly the silver stripes on the upholstery turned into steel bands that snapped shut over and around him. In one second, Paul found himself caged in steel bars. He screamed, but no one heard him.

He lay there, terrified, pushing against the bars without budging them in the least. He was trapped like an animal, and began to cry. Crying did no good, or calling out, or praying, but eventually he fell asleep still sobbing.

When he woke, it was in total darkness. He could feel his face sticky and smudged from his tears. He moved his arms, but could feel no bars around him. He sat up without difficulty, felt around, and realized he was in his own little bed. He didn't understand.

He got out of bed, noticed that he was still fully dressed but no shoes on, found the light. Everything normal. He peeked into his parents' bedroom and they seemed to be there, asleep too.

He wanted to go downstairs and eat something and have a lot of lights on and watch television, or anything, to get rid of his confusion. What had happened to him?

But he was, you know, a brave boy, so he opened the glass doors into the living room and went in. The street lamps outside seeping light in through the uncurtained windows let him see clearly enough, but he switched on the wall lights anyhow, hoping his parents wouldn't wake.

Where the sofa had been, there was a sofa still, but a different one, low and soft and mushy-cushy looking, grey, with a newspaper still lying on it. Paul did not understand. And there at one end of the sofa were the shoes he'd kicked off.

In the morning, at breakfast, nothing was said about what had happened. He was afraid to ask. At one point he felt courageous enough to remark that he liked the new sofa. His parents smiled at him, and went on talking about the meeting they'd been at the night before, something about politics.

The Seal Wife

THERE was a man who married a seal, as men of his island sometimes did. This man and his wife had this arrangement between them, that once a year, in the warm season, between Pentecost and Lammas, she would put on her old skin and take to the waves, and sport with her relations undersea, and see to such matters as seals have to concern them.

And so it went, year after year. Every August back she would come, slip out of her sleek wet fur, black with the water in it but brown when dry, and be a woman again, smile at him and put on Christian clothes and be a good wife. She'd be back just in time to help with the harvest and all the weary work that comes with it and more after.

He trusted her deeply, and never doubted her, and never speculated on what wickedness she might be up to deep in the sea or on the sunny rocks. What sin can a seal do, he thought, and was content with his certainty.

But one rainy summer he found himself missing her more than usual. If there was a week with a day of sun in it, it happened only once in that long stretch. The crops were in their soggy fields, and not much to do about it. The man spent much more time in their house than usual, thanks to the weather, and as he sat there day after day, missing her all the while, he fell to wondering what the life of a seal is really like. He thought it odd that he had never much bothered her with questions about that part of her life, and about the time before they had found each other on the beach and come together. He felt, and he was right to feel, that she didn't much like to be questioned about anything, least of all about the life they did not share. Full enough was her sharing in the life they had together most of the year.

That year she came back promptly, and more joyous than ever, not worried a bit about the bad weather and the crops, just happy to be home and with him. And he with her. And all went well, and the sky shifted and the sun came back and the fields dried out in time for a decent harvest.

When that was over and done with, they rested in the autumn, talked and drank cider and perry and looked at the sea. One day he couldn't help himself, though, and began to ask her.

What is it like, he wanted to know, the life you go down to every year, would I understand it if you told me? Ah, said she, that is the question, isn't it? Could I tell you, and could you understand? When I am a seal I do not have much use of language, and when I am a woman I'd have a long hard day of translation to put in words what happens without words. I am so happy with you, husband, do you really want to give me the pain of puting words to my knowledge?

No, no, said he, far from that. I am happy with you, just as we are. I was wondering only, when the rain came every day, and the air was like the sea itself, what it was like for you, darling, out there in it.

She smiled at him, and said no more. They ate their supper, porridge and yellow cheese, talked of this and that and went to their bed.

Next Sunday, when they came back from church and took off their uncomfortable Sunday clothes, she took him by the hand and led him down to the beach. They settled down on a nice old blanket on the shingle and watched the sea.

Husband, she said, I have been thinking of what you asked me — don't fret, I am not troubled by your question, I know it comes from love of me. I think I know a way of telling you what you want to know.

With that, she stood up and told him to take off his clothes. A little shyly, like most men of his island, he did as he was told. And she took off her clothes too. Naked as can be, she led him down to a big rock near just above high tide line, bent down and dug something out from beneath the rock.

Here, said she, put this on, and handed him a big shaggy dark skin of a seal. And no sooner had be begun to pull it over his head than the skin all by itself slipped down over his whole body snug as can be, and he flopped forward on the sand and was a seal.

She meantime had slipped into her own skin. Following her closely, he made his way with her into the waves, and soon found himself swimming almost without effort.

It felt as if the sea was swimming him, as if his body now needed to work hardly at all to keep moving, fast and sinuous, through the water.

For hours they cavorted, sometimes coming out and lying in the warm autumn sun, sometimes nuzzling tenderly. Then at one moment she swam beside him and nuzzled his little ear, and he could hear the thought forming, shall we go back now?

And suddenly he thought of labor, of harvest, of threshing, of winnowing, grinding grain, storing food, killing poor pigs and sheep and salting their meat, and that thought seemed horrible to him. And he thought of churches and schools and taverns, of travelers weary on the road and fishermen lost at sea, he thought of winter storms and summer heat, the blowflies on carrion and the thief at the door, he thought of old age and sickness and the parish cripple and the parish lunatic and the priest berating them for sins they scarcely had time to commit. And he thought to himself, I do not want to go back. Let me be with you here, forever.

His wife heard him, and rejoiced in her heart, for she had learned to love this man she had chanced to meet so many years ago.

Yes, my love, it will be as you say. And seals they were and seals they stayed to this very day. I can show you the empty house where they lived once, and nobody lives there now, since the people in the place have a vague feeling that the house belongs to somebody not far away.

Sometimes you can see husband and wife lying about on the sea rocks on a pleasant day, or sporting about a boat some child is paddling in the bay. How bright their eyes are, you can tell how happy they are.

Hillside

JAMES was tired. He'd been out walking in the little woods behind his house and had seen a deer. He tried to come close to it but the animal trotted away, and James decided to chase after it. And so he did. But when the deer reached the open fields beyond the trees, it really speeded up and James stumbled out, panting. Followed a little longer, but when the ground began to rise, he gave up the chase and sank down to catch his breath.

Lying there, he watched the sky, the clouds moving rather quickly, shaping and reshaping and passing by.

He may have dozed off for a few minutes, but came awake suddenly, feeling in his bones the presence of others. He sat up and saw a whole gang of people coming towards him, led by a young man playing a sort of guitar, but the sound box was shaped like half a watermelon. James couldn't hear the sound it made. The people's mouths and gestures made it seem they were singing, but James couldn't hear them either.

Even now as they came closer he heard nothing, not even their footsteps, even as they came right up and settled on the grass around him, close, close. He felt surrounded by these people, but they seemed to pay no attention to him. They settled down around him, taking their ease. A woman in a cocoa brown skirt sat so close to him that her leg pressed against his arm. She seemed to smile at him — but maybe not, James guessed, maybe she was smiling at the girl who had settled down on the other side of him — who smiled back, a smile that passed right over him.

All the while he heard nothing, not even their breaths, not even the rustle of their clothes. There must have been a dozen or more clustered around him on the hillside, seeming to talk and sing. James at first was afraid something was wrong with his ears, but when he scratched his check and tapped his forehead with a fingertip, he could hear those sounds just as usual.

The people were interesting to look at. They were handsome, all of them, in one way or another, young and pretty, old and noble, all worth looking at. Just below him, for example, a young man was facing him, evidently talking to the woman in brown beside James. The man had strong cheekbones, a high forehead, firm chin, and had carrot-red hair. James liked to look at pictures in art books, though he has never traveled to museums. But he saw something familiar in the man's face — Gosh, he said out loud, you look like a Greek statue!

He felt startled by having spoken, afraid of what the man might say or do. The man paid no attention, though something did happen. Something changed. Suddenly James could hear the chatter of their voices, and hear the fellow strumming on the big lute or whatever it was.

James could hear the voices clearly, but they were speaking a language he did not know, a language full of breathy vowels and sudden sharp consonants. James was about to be brave enough to ask questions, but the crowd began to fall silent, and began to rise up. He looked left and right, and the girl beside him did right then make eye-contact with him, and spoke, in English, laughing a little, mocking him prettily, maybe, licking her tongue out at him through heavily lip-sticked lips.

"You don't know who we are, do you? You are sitting on our roof. We live in the hill. Don't you know that every hill is inhabited? You people forget so easily." And she stuck her tongue at him, playful.

Just then an older man, who might have been her father, said "Growl!" in a loud voice. He didn't growl, he just said the word.

"Uh-oh," the girl said, "I'm talking too much, telling you too much — forget me."

And she leapt up with the others. As she rose, James caught a glimpse of the skin of her thigh, and it was white, white as... James thought of white things and finally decided, later, white as the keys on his mother's piano.

Meantime the girl and her friends hurried

down the hill, but then turned around and marched right into the ground. No door, no struggle, they just walked into the hillside and were gone.

The Rainbow

ONCE upon a time three girls were whiling away the summer afternoon in the barnyard, talking about their boyfriends real or proposed. A sudden squall came up over the prairie from the west with drenching rain. The girls hurried for shelter into the barn, careful not to smoke near the hay. The rain lasted only a few minutes, the storm cloud passed, and the girls came out into the sweet air the rain had freshened.

To their delight, they saw a big, very clear rainbow above them, with its great arch seeming to come to earth very nearby, just over the woodlot, or maybe even into the trees.

One girl started singing the rainbow song from The Wizard of Oz, and the other two giggled appreciatively. But she soon ran out of words, so they just watched the rainbow.

"I wonder if there really is a pot of gold at the end of the rainbow," one said, idly.

"But which end?" said the skeptic of the group, a girl on her third steady boyfriend, which gave her opinions weight. "Imagine traveling for years and getting there and finding out it was at the other end."

That left them glum for a few moments, and their thoughts were turning to other matters when the third girl said "But how close it looks! It seems to be coming down almost right here. Let's go and look!"

So off they went, carrying no provisions — how far could it be? They climbed the rail fence (straightest line to the nearby rainbow) and made their way across the cornfield. An onlooker would have seen three heads from time to time, or two, or just the head of the tallest girl, bouncing along, and would note the swooshing as if of small winds through the tall standing corn.

Once across the half-mile of field, they entered the small woodlot, expecting at any moment to see the darkness in among the trees light up with all the colors of the spectrum. And so they did, but not until they had walked deep into the woods, and one of the girls was already beginning to think of turning back, and another had actually whined a quiet how-long-are-we-supposed-to-go-on.

Then they were there. They stumbled into a clearing and there it was, the graceful arc blazing down its colors onto the brown earth. The girls were amazed, but felt no fear, somehow, and also felt no heat, for all the brightness before them.

And there were three young men in front of the rainbow, they seemed almost to be part of it, and the strange thing is that although they didn't seem to be wearing any clothes, they weren't naked either.

One young man, whose hair was yellow as corn and his skin ruddy, spoke first.

"Welcome, ladies of the prairie. We have come for you."

The second youth, curiously pale, almost greenish, lay on the ground and waved cheerfully. The third young man was very

dark, almost blue-black hair like a hero in a cartoon, and such dark skin! He too was smiling at the girls.

It was he who spoke next, very formally.

"It has come to our attention that women who reside on the prairie — itself part of the great circumglobal savannah or grassland, like those of Mongolia, the steppe of Central Asia, the puszta of Hungary — have more need of color than those who dwell in cities or jungles. Are we correct in so assuming?"

The girls didn't know what to say. One of them was thrilled to hear the word 'dwell' used in an actual spoken sentence, not in poetry. Another girl said, "I guess so…"

"So here we are," said Green from the ground, "which colors will be yours? I'm the simplest, but I cover the most ground. Roy here (pointing to the blond fellow who had first spoken) is fiery, hard to handle, but said to be a lot of fun. My blue bro Biv, he's moody, contemplative, a real philosopher, and no harm in him. Take your pick."

Now it so happened that each set of characteristics described appealed perfectly to the moods and wishes of one particular girl, so each girl knew at once her proper… proper what?

"What are you going to be to us," the skeptic asked, her eyes on Biv, "husbands, lovers, friends, teachers, children…?"

"Wait and see," answered Roy.

So with an inwardly breathed prayer of Whatever, the girls went to their chosen ones, and at the first embrace each girl fell asleep, and lay on the soft earth while the afternoon hummed away and the night came to know the prairie.

They woke when it was very dark, dark of the moon too, but the stars were clear enough, though the trees hid most of them. The girls woke all at the same time. No rainbow. They reached out and found each other, got up. They knew enough not to say anything. Curiously, they didn't miss the rainbow, or the young men. They felt oddly refreshed.

It didn't take them long to find their way home. The stars over the cornfield were magnificent, they'd never seemed so bright before, and in the twinkle of each the girls could see (but none of the three mentioned it) gleams and flickers of colors in the crystal white of their shine.

"We are very lucky ladies," one of the girls said.

"We know what we know," said the skeptic.

"We know who we are," said the third.

And when they got home each went to her bed, but all three of them went on dreaming this same dream that you and I are dreaming now. What color are you?

The Way to Fairyland

IT IS A well-known and often lamented fact that there is no way to get to Fairyland. No road leads the solitary traveler anywhere near it. But if one is taken there, led there by the hand of one who knows the way, then nothing is easier, no journey swifter. Every gap in the hedge, cleft between the rocks, any rickety old gate standing alone in an empty field, can lead you right in.

There was once a lonely young man who knew all that, and, like many young men, thought he knew better than what he knew. Many an afternoon he would spend apparently idling as it seems through woodland and meadow, but his eyes kept keen for that gateway he imagined into the land of the Fairies.

One day he had barely entered the wood, just in the first company of trees, where the meadow grasses and gold and purple weeds could still flourish in sunlight before the dim woods shadowed them to sleep. He walked along, looking down mostly, hoping for interesting mushrooms to nibble or walnuts to make dye from.

He heard a sound like a giggle or a chuckle, and saw a pretty girl sitting under a tree, her back against the trunk. She sat crosslegged, with her skirt spread neatly over her knees.

"Were you laughing?" the young man asked. "Indeed I was," she answered, still laughingly.

"I hope you weren't laughing at me," the boy said.

"Why should I laugh at you? You aren't the least bit funny looking, and you said nothing at all, neither funny nor sad. No, I was laughing at the way the sunlight coming through the leaves while the leaves are moving in the breeze made it look as if my lap were full of flowers."

The young man looked at the skirt, and could see that the light and dark, always moving, made interesting patterns, but they didn't remind him of flowers. So just to have something to say, he said:

"What kind of flowers are they?"

The girl's face looked serious at once. She reminded him of the way the schoolteacher looked when she was about to impart Important Information.

"There are blue heavenwhistles, and yellow don't-think-mes, and pink neverminds."

The boy had never heard of these flowers, so he said only hmmm.

She was a pretty girl, he recognized, not the prettiest girl he'd ever seen in church or carnival or in his dreams, but pretty enough. But by now she was staring back into her spread skirt, her eyes gleaming and moving about as if she were watching goldfish in a pond. He couldn't think of anything to say, so he moved on, wandering among some saplings, not expecting much from such new growth.

After it might have been half an hour, he began to wish he could see the girl again, so he tried to make his way back to her directly. It took longer than he expected, because he found himself moving (to judge by sunlight and shadows) in the right direction, but through unfamiliar trees and bushes. He was sure she'd be gone by the time he got back to her tree.

But when he finally stumbled out of some unexpectedly tough and close-grown tall grasses and into the clearing where she'd been, he saw her still there. And to his surprise, he saw her lap full of flowers.

"O there are flowers there!" he cried out. "I see them now."

"I thought you might," said the girl. "Come!"

And with that she tossed one of the blue flowers at him. He caught it in midair, and when he looked back at her she was standing, and no flowers to be seen. "Come," she said again.

She reached out her left hand. The boy took it with his right hand. She looked him in the eye, very serious, then turned her head and led him along through the trees.

Left with right
day and night
hold me tight
and if you dare
we'll soon be there

she sang as they went along, and he liked well the tune, and the words even better. Soon they came to a strange looking thing, an old door in its door frame, but no house to it, not even a wall. The whole business looked as if it would fall to pieces any minute.

For the first time since she'd been leading him, she turned to face him.

"Are you sure?" she asked, simply, as if she'd asked him for the time of day and he'd guessed at it.

Am I sure? the young man thought. I think that's all I really am, he thought.

"I am sure," he said, trying to make his voice ordinary, but there was some sort of boast or triumph in it.

The girl looked away, and still holding him with her left hand, opened the door with her right, and pulled him through.

And that is how he came to be in Fairyland, and it is not right to tell of what he found there, and what it was like, or how long he stayed, or if he ever came home. What we can know for certain was the smile of surprise and joy on his face as he walked through the door and looked around from right to left.

IN ADDITION to many books of poetry and essays, **ROBERT KELLY** has published five collections of short fiction (all from McPherson & Co.); a book of plays (*Oedipus After Colonus*); several novels (most recently *The Work of the Heart*); and new poetry: *Calls*; *The Secret Name of Now*; and *Reasons to Resist*. A large collection of his essays, *A Voice Full of Cities*, has recently been matched by *A City Full of Voices*, studies of his work by many writers. He teaches in the Written Arts Program at Bard College.

EMMA O'DONNELL POLYAKOV studied art at Bard College, and currently teaches and writes about religion. She is Assistant Professor of Religious and Theological Studies at Merrimack College, and the author of *The Nun in the Synagogue: Judeocentric Catholicism in Israel* and *Remembering the Future: The Experience of Time in Jewish and Christian Liturgy*, and the editor of *Antisemitism, Islamophobia, and Interreligious Hermeneutics: Ways of Seeing the Religious Other.*